DACI

Notebook

This Book Belongs To

Made in United States
Orlando, FL
27 November 2024

54554544R00068